You Can Be a Good Friend
(No Matter What!)
A LIL TJ BOOK

TARAJI P. HENSON

ILLUSTRATED BY PAUL KELLAM

To my dear, sweet grandma Patsie Ballard. —TPH
For Kiley: I admire all your many quirks, lil sis, always stay true to yourself. —PK

ZONDERKIDZ
You Can Be a Good Friend (No Matter What!)
Copyright © 2024 by Taraji P. Henson
Illustrations © 2024 Taraji P. Henson

Published in Grand Rapids, Michigan, by Zonderkidz. Zonderkidz is a registered trademark of The Zondervan Corporation, L.L.C., a wholly owned subsidiary of HarperCollins Christian Publishing, Inc.

Requests for information should be addressed to customercare@harpercollins.com.

ISBN 978-0-310-16059-5 (hardcover)
ISBN 978-0-310-16073-1 (audio)
ISBN 978-0-310-16072-4 (ebook)
ISBN 978-0-310-16801-0 (signed hardcover)
ISBN 978-0-310-16800-3 (signed carton)

Publisher's Note: This is a work of fiction. Names, characters, places, and incidents are either products of the author's imagination or used fictitiously. All characters are fictional, and any similarity to people living or dead is purely coincidental.

No part of this publication may be reproduced, stored in a retrieval system, or transmitted in any form or by any means—electronic, mechanical, photocopy, recording, or any other—except for brief quotations in printed reviews, without the prior permission of the publisher.

Zondervan titles may be purchased in bulk for educational, business, fundraising, or sales promotional use. For information, please email SpecialMarkets@Zondervan.com.

Illustrated by Paul Kellam
Editor: Katherine Jacobs
Interior Design: Kristen Sasamoto

Printed in Malaysia
24 25 26 27 28   IMG   5 4 3 2 1

Lil TJ was one cool kid. She had funky style, groovy rhythm, and the most magnificent dog anyone anywhere had ever seen.

Lil TJ's Grandma Patsy lived far away but TJ talked to Grandma almost every day. She told Grandma everything—her hopes, her dreams, her adventures with Willie. And lately, TJ had been telling her all about school starting and how she was going to make a million friends.

Grandma said, "Remember, friendships take time, Baby Girl. You need to nurture them to help them grow."

Finally! It was the first day of school! Lil TJ woke up extra early, put on her best outfit, did her hair, and packed her backpack. She was ready!

"Are you nervous, little sis?" her big brother Keith asked.

"Nervous? Why would I be nervous??" Lil TJ practically shouted. "I'm going to learn a bunch of new things, eat lunch in a real lunchroom, play on a big playground, and make some new friends!"

Keith gave TJ a quick hug as he grabbed breakfast and ran out the door for his first day of school too.

As Lil TJ walked into school, she did her best to hide her first-day jitters. "This is going to be so much fun," she whispered to herself as she took a deep breath.

TJ loved her new teacher. And her desk was right up front and center!

In music class she got to try a bunch of instruments, including a *real* recorder.

And during art class she drew the most beautiful picture of Willie she had ever created.

At recess time TJ was ready to go outside to talk, laugh, and make some new friends, but as the class lined up to go outside, someone bumped into her.

It was a boy named Beau. "You're so little, I almost stepped on you!" he shouted.

Lil TJ looked around at the other kids. No one said anything.

After that it felt like everything Lil TJ did bothered Beau. He did not like her drawings of Willie at all.

"What kind of animal is *that*, TJ? A hippo?" Beau whispered.

TJ decided not to hang her picture on the "Share Board."

While TJ was talking to Cindy, Beau leaned over. "Don't you have an inside voice?"

And at lunchtime Beau made a funny face when he saw Lil TJ eating her absolute favorite sandwich—peanut butter and tomato. "Eww! That's so weird!" he yelled. TJ tucked her sandwich under her napkin. She wasn't hungry anymore.

Lil TJ had never felt so sad, lonely, and confused. Where were her million new friends? Even Willie's beautiful face couldn't make her feel better.

At school TJ tried not to attract Beau's attention. She wore her plainest clothes. She did her hair like the other girls. And she ate regular peanut butter and jelly just like the others.
But her tummy still had big, nervous butterflies.

She was so nervous, she couldn't help beating her pencil on the desk and tapping her foot as she worked on her worksheet. Beau whispered in a loud voice, "Quit the tapping, TJ!"

TJ wished she could shrink and disappear. Maybe making new friends wasn't worth it after all.

Lil TJ told Grandma Patsy how school was going. "I think I made a bully instead of a friend, Grandma. I tried so hard!"

"Oh, Baby Girl," Grandma Patsy said. "You've heard me say 'You get more flies with honey,' haven't you? Now's the time! Be honey—show them your sweet self. You can be a good friend no matter what!"

TJ had a lot to think about after that call. How could she be a good friend to Beau and everyone else?

The next day TJ put on her favorite outfit, did her hair in her favorite style, and packed her favorite sandwich.
 She waved to Beau on the bus—reminding herself to be sweet like honey.

When her teacher asked a question, she sat up tall and raised her hand high with all the other kids.

Recess time still felt hard, though, and Lil TJ just wanted to be alone. So when everyone else went to the playground, TJ headed to the music room.

She sat for a few minutes in the peace and quiet.

She squeaked a recorder.

Then she tried a trombone.

She plunked at the piano.

And then she sat down at the big, shiny set of drums. Ping, ping, clash, crash, boom, bang . . . Without missing a beat, Lil TJ felt like she was getting happier, braver, and more sure of herself.

Soon kids from the playground came inside to join the fun!

Squawk! From across the room came the most awful sound.

Beau was holding a violin, trying hard to act as though he knew exactly what he was doing. But with each new and loud screech his face got redder. And he looked like he had big, nervous butterflies in his tummy.

Lil TJ remembered Grandma Patsy's words: "Friendships take time. You need to nurture them to help them grow."

"Be sweet like honey," she whispered to herself as she went to sit next to Beau.

"Close your eyes, Beau. Take two big breaths,"
TJ said as she smiled at Beau.

In . . . out.

In . . . out.

TJ and Beau breathed together.
Then Beau surprised TJ.

"I'm sorry, TJ," Beau said. "I've been pretty mean to you. Sometimes new things make me nervous and I don't know what to do. You aren't like anyone else I've ever met! So I wasn't very nice."

"You aren't like anyone else I have ever met either, Beau! But maybe that's a good thing. We can be special together. Now, start playing that violin!" she said, and went back to the drums.

"One, two, three, four!" TJ counted off. And soon the children were creating beautiful music together as one, big group—as friends!

A NOTE FROM TARAJI

There is nothing you would not do to protect your child. While they are young, we can create a bubble of protection around them. But at some point, we must release them to the world and pray this world is kind to them. Unfortunately, bullying of some sort is something that all children are likely to encounter at some point in their life. And when it happens to your own child, you may feel angry, stressed, and find it difficult to concentrate on anything else. All you want is to make the bullying stop. Although you may feel helpless, there are things you can and should do. If you suspect your child is being bullied:

1. **Provide Support and Love on Your Child:** Before doing anything else, it is important your child feels loved and supported. Let them know how much you love and care about them and how important they are. Create a safe environment for them to share more details about their experiences with you. Give them time, as this is often not easy.

2. **Listen to Your Child and Document Everything:** Ask open-ended questions and get as much information as you can. Details are very important. Document dates, times, places, actions, and threats. Print out emails and text messages and take pictures or screenshots of social media posts.

3. **Become an Expert on Bullying:** Every school has anti-bullying policies, and all 50 states now have anti-bullying laws. Become familiar with these so you know your rights and what steps to take to report a situation. If bullying is happening at school, you generally report it to your child's school. If bullying is happening online or outside of school, you should report it to the police. If cyberbullying is occurring, you can report it to the Internet Service Provider, social media website, or wherever it is taking place.

4. **Be Persistent:** Become part of the plan to stop the bullying. Ask the school principal what you can do to help. Document what authorities have agreed to do and hold them accountable. Talk to your child to determine if things have improved. If not, you may have to escalate your complaints (e.g., superintendent of schools, board of education, state authorities, etc.).

5. **Engage Professional Mental Health Support:** The experience of being bullied can take a psychological toll on a child, affecting their emotional, mental, and physical health. Because this experience can be traumatic for everyone involved, enlisting mental health support as early as possible can help to prevent long-lasting consequences and provide you and your child with coping strategies to help them heal.

For more information about my mental health organization, go to borislhensonfoundation.org.